Christmas in Water Village

Paintings
by
Jean
Colquhoun

Story
by
Christine
Maxfield

To Joanne,

Merry Christmas!
1990

Christine Maxfield

Published by Prima Design

Published by Prima Design
Water Village
New Hampshire 03864

Design by P. M. Hodder
Printed in Hong Kong
First Edition

Library of Congress Catalog Card Number 89-60716

ISBN 0-962-10290-3

The art consists of oil paintings that
are reproduced in full color.

To my wonderful family

L ong ago, when I was a child in Water Village, my brother Joshua and I lived near town in a house on a hill with Mother and Father.

In Spring we caught fish from the brook, in summer we jumped from haystacks and in autumn we climbed apple trees from which we would pick the crisp sweet fruits. But as with children everywhere, our favorite time of year was Christmas.

Christmas meant the beginning of winter. There were skating parties and sleigh rides, cold noses and hot cider, mistletoe and secrets. There were many children in Water Village then, and we were all friends.

Then one day, a new little girl came to our school. We were making a big paper star to decorate the classroom as Christmas was only two weeks away. Our teacher brought the little girl in and introduced her as Hannah; she would only look down at her feet, her honey colored hair falling over her face as she walked to a corner of the room and sat down. We asked her to play with us but she would only shake her head. Days passed and we became used to her silence.

One cold darkening afternoon, Joshua and I ran home from school, stopping by to see Father in his workshop. He was a cooper and the barrels he made were sold to a factory in Portsmouth, a city by the sea.

"Hullo Joshua, hullo Patience!" Father said as he ruffled the hair on the top of our heads with his strong hands. He returned to his workbench and began to saw a large flat piece of wood; Thomas, his apprentice, smiled at us as he pounded nails into the top of a barrel. Joshua and I picked up a hoop Father had made for us to play with and, using little sticks, we rolled it back and forth across the room. Suddenly the hoop crashed into Father. He grabbed it and said, "Off to your mother, and see to your chores!" But there was a twinkle in his eye as he shooed us away.

The frigid snow squeaked under our feet as we ran out of the workshop towards the animal shed. As we did every year, Joshua and I had set out a little Christmas tree for our few animals. I gave our horse Lucky an apple from the storage bin, and Adam, Thomas' little boy, gave one to our donkey. We swept out their pens and gave them fresh water and food.

"Joshua, come!" I said when we were finished. "Mother must be just taking the bread from the oven." We quickly shut the barn door and dashed home across the field.

11

H ullo, my children," Mother said as she gently gave each of us a kiss. There was a fire blazing in the hearth. My mouth watered as I watched Mother slice pieces of her fluffy warm bread and put them on plates for us. We waited eagerly as she took butter and raspberry jam from the cupboard and set them in front of us.

Then Mother said, "I have heard there is a new girl named Hannah at school and that she has no friends."

"She doesn't talk," Joshua said as he wiped a bit of jam off his cheek.

"She's a very sad girl, Joshua," Mother continued. "Her father, Captain Fisher, has been lost at sea; it means that no one knows where he or his ship is, and perhaps no one will ever see him again. Little Hannah's mother is feeling poorly and hasn't been able to keep up with her sewing. It's all she has to provide for herself and Hannah."

Joshua and I looked at each other. "Oh, Mother," I exclaimed. "Poor Hannah."

Mother continued quietly as she began to pack butter, jam and fresh bread into a basket, "Mrs. Fisher had to sell their fine house in Portsmouth and move out here to the country with Hannah. It's just the two of them now, you see. They board at Mrs. Wiggins' house."

Joshua and I frowned. We did not like Mrs. Wiggins. None of the children in Water Village did. She was very old and wrinkled and bent over. We thought she was a witch. She lived in a big yellow house with two chimneys, down a way from the stone bridge, and always had a room to let.

"Please leave early for school tomorrow morning so that you"ll have time to deliver this basket to Mrs. Fisher," Mother said as she placed a large red napkin over the basket and put it on the hutch by the door.

Our eyes grew large. "But Mother! Mrs. Wiggins is so scary. She'll probably chase us out with a broom!" I cried. Mother returned to the table, put her arms around our shoulders reassuringly and said "My dears, Mrs. Wiggins is simply a lonely old lady who can't hear very well. She means you no harm."

The next morning Joshua and I, laden with the basket, trudged through the snow to Mrs. Wiggins' house. "Maybe we could just leave the basket at the door and run," Joshua suggested.

"No, Joshua," I said. "Old Mrs. Wiggins would probably keep it and eat it all herself!"

We giggled at the thought, but our steps slowed when we finally reached the path that led to Mrs. Wiggins' door. I was just tall enough to reach the knocker. I slammed it hard two times and stepped back.

"Well, well! Joshua and Patience Jewell!" Mrs. Wiggins cackled as she opened the door, bending over and squinting at us.

I took a deep breath and said, "Mrs. Wiggins, our mother has sent a basket of food for Mrs. Fisher."

"What? What?" Mrs. Wiggins bent over even closer and shouted, "You children mumble so!"

I held the basket up and shouted back. "This is for Mrs. Fisher!"

"Oh my, how nice!" Mrs. Wiggins suddenly smiled a bright toothless smile. Perhaps she wasn't so scary after all. "Come right this way, children," she said as we followed her down a long hallway. Mrs. Wiggins knocked on a door and Hannah opened it, quickly hiding something behind her back when she saw us.

"Hello, dear. Some friends are here to pay an early morning call," Mrs. Wiggins said.

"Do come in!" said a voice from within. We all entered the small sunny room. Hannah's mother was sitting on a chair with a blanket across her lap. She was younger and prettier than I had imagined, but very pale.

"Good morning, Mrs. Fisher," I said. "We are Joshua and Patience Jewell. Our mother asked us to bring you this." I held out the basket and smiled.

"Thank you so very much Patience. Put it over there, please." She did not stand but gestured towards a table which held a tiny Christmas tree decorated with bits of lace.

"Hannah, isn't it nice of Patience and Joshua to call on us? Do sit down and visit with us." We sat, and Joshua asked "What have you got there behind you, Hannah?" He craned his neck trying to see.

Slowly Hannah pulled out a doll with the loveliest china face and honey colored curls. "What a beautiful doll you have!" I exclaimed.

"Father brought it to me from London, all the way across the ocean. Her name is Emma," she said proudly. "I can't wait to see what he'll bring me this time. He's been gone ever so long."

I saw Mrs. Wiggins and Mrs. Fisher exchange sad looks, but I was very happy that Hannah had finally spoken to us. As I admired Emma, Joshua asked, "Mrs. Fisher, are you feeling better today?"

"Yes, Joshua, I am better, thanks to people like your mother who have offered us so much help and friendship, and we hope to join you all at the family social Saturday night, don't we Hannah?" Hannah again looked shyly to the floor.

"Oh Hannah, you must go!" I exclaimed. "We'll sing Christmas carols on the common while we light candles on the town tree. Then we'll skate on the Indian River holding election torches, and oh, the big supper! And I love to watch the grown-ups dance."

A smile flickered across Hannah's lips. Joshua added, "And at the end of the evening there are presents for all of us!" The corners of Hannah's mouth curled up some more.

I stood up. "We should go on to school now, Hannah. Will you walk with us?"

She nodded and gently placed her precious Emma on a chair. The three of us skipped off after saying good-bye to Mrs. Wiggins and to Hannah's mother.

That evening, my family and I decorated the big spruce tree father had chopped down and put in the keeping room.

I felt so warm and happy, but at the same time, I couldn't help thinking about Hannah and her mother; how sad it must be without a father and without a home any more. I considered Mrs Fisher to be quite a strong and brave woman.

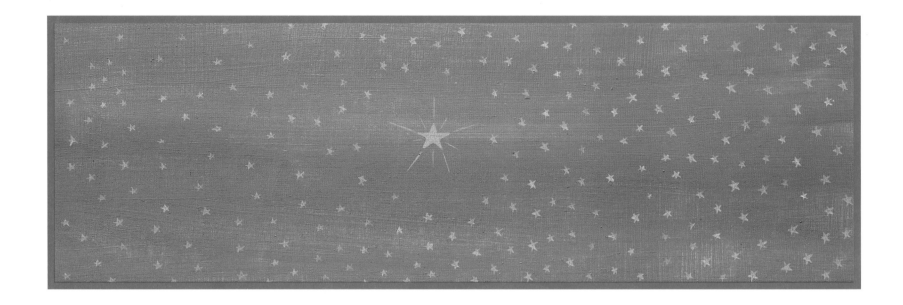

I looked out the window and saw a star, a very bright star like the Christmas Star of ages ago, rising in the blue-black sky. That special star had guided the three wise men on their journey to find the baby Jesus. Could there be a star for Captain Fisher? Perhaps it was guiding him homeward now. I wished with all my might that Captain Fisher would soon be found. Someone in Portsmouth could tell him where his family had gone. I could picture him, waiting in some distant land for the ship that would deliver him safely home.

The next morning was a busy one with cakes to bake and presents to wrap for the family social that night. There was a rustling, bustling, giddy excitement about the house which always happened at Christmas time.

Finally, Mother cried, "Enough! Let's be off to the common now!"

Jean Colquhouri

We all bundled up and packed our goods into the sleigh. Father clucked gently to Lucky and soon we were trotting through the frosty air to carols and candles and friends.

There were many friends and neighbors singing along in the bandstand on the common. But I didn't see Hannah or her mother. I hoped that I would soon see them at the Indian River Grange Hall.

And sure enough, they were there! Hannah had remembered her skates and we raced upon the ice, hooting and hollering with all the children until the grown-ups called us in for supper. We eagerly dashed inside to the warm brightness of the Christmas party.

Once there, with the happy noise of the townspeople, Hannah again became sad. She took a slice of bread from the table which was overflowing with wonderful foods and stood alone behind the big Christmas tree.

She stared down at the many presents, her eyes moist, unsmiling. I spoke to her and she shook her head the way she used to when we first met.

After supper, the children settled down around the tree, but not Hannah. She stood away, staring blankly at a frosty window. It was all so still and quiet, even the babies were hushed. I'll never forget what happened next. We all heard the sound of big boots stamping outside the door.

Everyone turned his head as the door slowly opened, letting in a gust of cold wind and a whirl of glistening snow. A tall, broad man walked in. He removed his hat and shook snow from it, revealing his face and his honey colored hair.

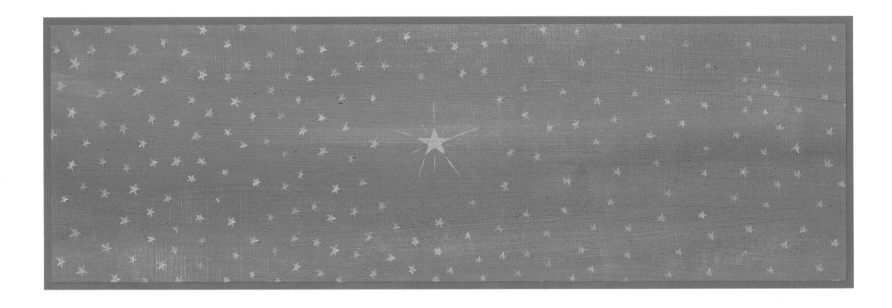

I heard a child cry "Father!" I looked at Hannah's face. I thought of what happens when a cloud slips past the sun, allowing its radiance to fill the world again.

"Father!" she cried as she ran across the room. She buried herself in his arms.

My Christmas wish was granted! Hannah's father had returned.

We all clapped and cheered, the women dabbed at their eyes and the men slapped each other on the back. Mother sat down at the piano and began to play "Joy to the World". Filled with the spirit of love, we all sang out so loudly that I imagine people heard us down to Portsmouth!

Hannah and I are old now, but we're still close friends. We often reminisce about that magical Christmas long ago when a little girl's wish came true. Now, when the snow is so cold that it squeaks under our boots, and the big evergreen tree is decorated in the Grange Hall, we love to tell the story to our grandchildren, at Christmas time.